RUBBLE GHOST

BY JILLIAN POWELL
ILLUSTRATED BY PETER RICHARDSON

FULL FLIGHT

Titles in the Full Flight Thrills and Spills series:

The Knight Olympics	Jonny Zucker
Pied Piper of London	Danny Pearson
The Science Project	Jane A C West
Gorilla Thriller	Richard Taylor
Clone Zone	Jillian Powell
Clowning Around	Helen Orme
Time to go Home	David Orme
Haunted Car	Roger Hurn
Dinosaur Rampage	Craig Allen
Rubbish Ghost	Jillian Powell

Badger Publishing Limited
Oldmedow Road,
Hardwick Industrial Estate,
King's Lynn PE30 4JJ
Telephone: 01438 791037
www.badgerlearning.co.uk

4 6 8 10 9 7 5

Rubbish Ghost ISBN 978 1 84926 989 6

Text © Jillian Powell 2013
Complete work © Badger Publishing Limited 2013
Second edition © 2014

Publisher: Susan Ross
Senior Editor: Danny Pearson
Designer: Fiona Grant
Illustrator: Peter Richardson

Contents

New words:

haunted	damp
shipped	loomed
ghostly	creaked
floated	complained
glide	vanished

Main characters:

Josh

Saffi

The Ghost

CHAPTER 1

Bad News

"So there it is," Lord Flippit said. "I am sorry to say, the house will have to close."

The staff looked glum.

Josh and Saffi loved their jobs at Abbey Manor. Josh helped out in the kitchens. One day he hoped to be a cook. Saffi led tours around the house on Saturdays. The tips were helping her save up money for singing lessons.

"There must be some way of getting the house to make money!" Saffi said.

Lord Flippit shook his head. "We have tried everything I am afraid," he told them. "Weddings, music gigs, open garden days. None of them brings in enough money. The roof needs work. There is damp in the walls. It is a sad day but we are going to have to sell up. It is such an old house, such a very old house…"

"Old house…! Wait, I've got an idea!" Josh said.

"What Abbey Manor needs is a ghost!
Ghost tours are really popular.
If people think Abbey Manor is
haunted, we will get loads of visitors.
We can invite ghost hunters and ghost
busters and have creepy weekends
and…"

Lord Flippit put up his hand.
"Brilliant idea, Josh, just one small
problem. Ghosts don't grow on trees do
they? Ghosts just… appear. Where
would you get a ghost from?"

Josh looked at Saffi.

"The internet!" Saffi said brightly. "You
can get anything on the internet Sir!"

"Really?" Lord Flippit said. He was not really into computers.

"Leave it with us, sir," Josh said boldly. "If you think it's a good idea?"

"I think it's a great idea!" Lord Flippit said. "Our very own ghost, pulling in the tours. Josh and Saffi, you are in charge. Go find us a ghost!"

CHAPTER 2

Ghost Shopping

"Here we go!" Josh said, looking at the screen. "'Ghosts Galore', that sounds like a good website."

He clicked the mouse.

"Wow! Look at all those ghosts!" Saffi said. "That one looks good! Look, she carries her head under her arm!"

"What about this one?" Josh said. "He drags chains along behind him. There's a sound button so you can hear the noise it makes. Listen!" Josh clicked on the sound button and they could hear the sound of wailing and clanking chains.

It certainly made Josh feel spooked.

"That's really scary!" Saffi said.

"Think of all the places he could drag his chains round in the Manor!" Josh said.

"It would be really creepy hearing that. Let's find out how much he costs."

Josh clicked to add the ghost to the shopping cart.

"What? We can't afford that!" Saffi said. "That's more than double what we have to spend. Try the one with the head under her arm. She might be a bit cheaper."

Josh clicked the mouse and updated the cart. "She costs even more!" he said. "This is pants. A ghost could bring in the money but we can't afford to buy one!"

"Wait, it says 'Bargain buys' there," Saffi pointed out.

"Bargain buys? How can you have a bargain ghost?" Josh clicked the mouse again.

"Oh, I see. They are beginners," Saffi said. "Look, there are First Years, Second Years. They are just starting out as ghosts."

"Better try a First Year, they will be cheapest!" Josh said.

"What about that one?" Saffi said, pointing at the screen. "It says 'Total Beginner. Willing to learn. Ready now.'"

"'Ready now' feels like we're buying a puppy!" Josh said. "Still, look, he is really cheap."

"Anyway, a ghost is a ghost," Saffi said. "If this one does well and we get loads of ghost tours, Lord Flippit will be able to afford an upgrade!

"OK, let's do it!" Josh said. He added the ghost to the cart and went to check out.

"That's it! We've done it," Josh said. "Look, it says 'Shipped. Expect in three to five days.'"

Now all they had to do was wait for the ghost to appear.

CHAPTER 3

Scary – Not!

Josh and Saffi were sitting on the steps of the Manor. "They said up to five days. It's been seven days now," Saffi said.

"Did you just hear a knock at the door?" Josh looked around.

"Josh, we are sitting outside," Saffi said. "Who knocks a front door from the inside?"

They looked at each other. Josh opened the door. It was the ghost.

"You're late!" Saffi said.

"Sorry about that," the ghost said. "I went to the Abbey by mistake."

"The Abbey is just a pile of stones!" Josh said.

"With five ghosts living there," the ghost told them. "Very friendly ghosts. We got chatting and…"

"Yes, well, you're here now," Josh said. "The thing is, next week we have a big tour group coming. They are ghost hunters. They want to see the Abbey Manor ghost. That's where you come in. They want to be scared! Can you help us?"

"OK," the ghost said. "Where do I start?"

"Well, how about you show us what you can do?" Saffi said. "How about making a scary noise?"

"OK, here goes…whoooo…whooooo… woooooooo."

"That sounds like a party popper!" Josh said. "Is that the best you can do?"

"Sorry!" the ghost said. "I am a beginner. Did they tell you?"

"Never mind," Saffi said. "You do look ghostly. At least that's something. How about walking through a wall? That would be good."

The ghost nodded and floated off towards a wall.

SMACK!! CRASH!!! He crashed straight into the wall and stood, rubbing his nose.

"Maybe that needs work," Josh said, looking at Saffi.

"Look, you could glide down the stairs," Saffi said. "That would look really scary."

"These stairs? OK" the ghost said.
He floated to the top and began
coming down.

"That's good!" Josh said.

The ghost looked pleased. He went to
give them the thumbs-up but he lost
his balance. He tripped and fell all the
way down, landing in a big heap at the
bottom of the stairs.

"This is a really rubbish ghost!" Josh said to Saffi.

The ghost was just getting up when Lord Flippit's little dog ran in.

"Hey, dogs are scared of ghosts, this could be good!" Saffi said.

Pooch began barking, his tiny tail wagging. The ghost looked really afraid, and vanished.

CHAPTER 4

Ghost Training

They found him in the toilet. "Sorry about that. I've never been keen on dogs," he told them.

"That dog is not scary. He is so small you can put him in a handbag!" Saffi said.

"Look, you have to man-up… well, ghost-up," Josh told him. "The ghost tour is our last chance. The ghost hunters are expecting big things. It is up to you to save the Manor!"

The ghost gulped.

"I think you can do it," Saffi said. "You just need some training."

The ghost's eyes lit up.

"That's more like it!" Saffi said. "Your eyes look quite scary!"

"Really?" The ghost looked pleased.

Ghost training started the next day. They began with the wall. The ghost tried a few times. "These walls are so thick!" he complained, rubbing his nose.

"It's not just the walls that are thick!" Josh said to Saffi.

The ghost tried again. "Look, look, I am doing it!" he said.

"He's right. He's going through the wall!" Saffi said. "Keep going, that's it!"

But that was it. For the next hour, the ghost was stuck in the wall. He could not go any further. In the end, he had to back up.

Josh and Saffi were starting to worry.

"Let's try something else," Josh said.
"The bedrooms have four-poster beds.
You can hide behind the curtain and
jump out. The ghost hunters will
love that."

They took the ghost up to a bedroom
and left him inside.

"We will go out and come in again,"
Josh said. "When you hear us, just
jump out and make a scary noise."

They went out and came back in a
few moments later. The bed curtains
were closed. They waited to be spooked
by the ghost.

"What's that noise?" Saffi said. They
went over to the bed.

Josh pulled back the curtain. The ghost was fast asleep, snoring.

"This is hopeless, or rather this ghost is hopeless!" Josh said.

"We can't give up!" Saffi told him. "The ghost tour is booked. We have to make this work."

"I know," Josh said. "But with this rubbish ghost can we do it in time?"

CHAPTER 5

The Big Event

The day of the tour had come. The ghost hunters were in the big hall. They all wanted to see the Abbey Manor ghost. Saffi was leading the tour around the house.

The tour began after dark to try and make it extra scary. Saffi and Josh carried lamps.

"The Manor is more than four hundred years old," she told the group as they went up the stairs. The stairs creaked. Shadows loomed.

The house really did feel rather creepy in the dark.

They came to a bedroom and Saffi opened the door. She looked at Josh. This was where they had told the ghost to be.

Inside the room, they felt a sudden chill and the lamps almost went out.

"What was that?" someone said. "Something went past me!"

There was a sudden rush of air as a window blew open. The bed curtains parted and something moved across the room. The lamps went out. When they came on again, someone screamed.

"It's there! I saw it, in the mirror. It's the ghost of Abbey Manor!"

Outside on the landing, a chair began rocking. A vase fell from a table and smashed. Pooch appeared then shot downstairs with his tail between his legs.

Saffi looked at Josh. This was getting a bit too real! Still, the ghost hunters were thrilled. By the time they left, the Manor had tours booked well into the next year.

"That was brill!" Saffi said to Josh. "Where is the ghost? We had better go and thank him."

They looked everywhere. Then Josh heard a small sound coming from a cupboard. He opened the door.

"What are you doing in there?" Saffi asked.

"Sorry," the ghost said. "It was all those people. They were a bit scary."

"You mean you've been in here all the time?" Josh said. He looked at Saffi. "Well if he was in here... then who… or what, was upstairs?"

"The Abbey Manor ghost!" they both said together.

"Well… it looks like the Manor is safe now, and our jobs too!" Saffi said.

"What about my job?" the ghost asked them.

"Well… you need lessons and now you can learn from a real ghost!" Josh said.

"WHOO WHOOOO!"

He still sounded like a party popper.

Ghost Jokes

Here are some really ghostly jokes to try out on your friends!

What kind of street does a ghost live on?
A dead end.

Why can't ghosts tell lies?
Because you can see right through them.

When do ghosts usually appear?
Just before someone screams.

Why did the ghost cross the road?
To get to 'The Other Side'.

What kind of mistakes do ghosts make?
Boo boos.

What do you call a ghost's mother and father?
Transparents.

Who is the most important player on a ghosts' football team?
The ghoulie.

Where do ghosts like to go swimming?
The Dead Sea.

Who did the ghost invite to his party?
Anyone he could dig up.

What did one ghost say to another?
Do you believe in people?

What do ghosts like eating?
Spookgetti.

What do ghosts play at parties?
Hide and shriek.

Questions about the Story

Why did Abbey Manor have to close?

Why does Saffi need her job at the Manor?

Why does the ghost turn up late?

Why does the ghost hide in the cupboard?

What makes one of the ghost hunters scream?

What was the name of Lord Flippit's dog?

Do you believe in ghosts?